Life is a Journey

Life is a Journey

By

Mary Minjeur

Ordering Information:

For orders and inquiries, please contact:
1-888-375-9818
www.toplinkpublishing.com
bookorder@toplinkpublishing.com

Printed in the United States of America

Dedication...

"In manus Dei... In God's hands..."
Whatever the outcome—it is God's will.
And so... I dedicate this book
to all who were part of my travels,
to my husband, Carel,
my mentor and my best friend,
and to my beloved, growing
family who I love dearly.
I offer my life to Jesus, my Lord and Savior,
As my Journey to Him continues...

Mary

CONTENTS

Events to Try One's Soul

Alicia's Courage 3

Incarcerated 4

I've Lost My Poem...5

Pandemonium 6

The Corn Maze 7

The Eyes Have It..8

The Languor Of The Drink 9

When Children Leave Home 10

Life's Journeys and U-turns

A Sibling's Journey Back In Time................................13

Culpable 14

Life—An Ancient Scroll? 15

Life Is A Journey Home 16

The Great Divide 17

Love Conquers All

A Love Story 21

A Moment's Despair...22

Love Smothers Differences 23

Divine Fortune—25 25

Taken For The Taking...27

The Marriage Blessing Of Carel And Monica 28

The Wedding Blessing For Patrick And Ann 31

When Love Comes 32

Precious Moments

The Miracle 35

Life Is But A Breath 36

Pat's Soliloquy 37

Every Day Is Friday 38

Farewell Little Bird 39

Revelations Of The Mind 40

Happy St. Patrick's Day 41

The Cottage 42

The Beauty of the Earth and the Majesty of God

Beauty In Chaos 45

Does God Visit The Earth 46

The Magnificent Earth 48

Of Dusk 50

The Sorrows of the Heart

Broken 52

Ghost Writer 53

Driftwood 54

Empty Echoes 56

Shalom… Peace 57

Shards Of Conviction 58

Signs Of Disparity 59

Subtle Burdens 60

Will They Put Flowers On My Grave 61

Worth 62

Tragedies

Dementia..64

Different Generations 65

I Know I Don't Know... 66

Thanksgiving With Mom 68

The Birthday I Didn't Want To Remember............. 69

We Live by Faith

Bring Us Back O Lord! 73

Eternity Begins Now.. 74

Hope... 76

Lamentations..77

Mary, Lady Of The Salvation Army........................ 78

My God In The Shower 80

Psalm Of Submission.. 81

The Innocuous Compromising Of Our Values........ 82

Where Are You God? 84

The Grace To Return.. 85

The Rescue of Sammy

The Rescue Of Sammy... 90

Events to Try One's Soul

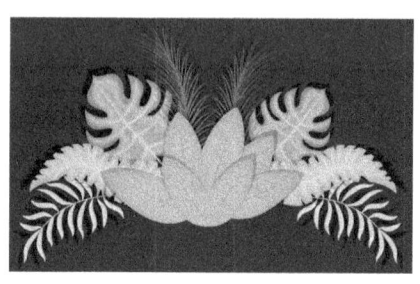

Joy is not in things,

it is in us.

Benjamin Franklin

ALICIA'S COURAGE

I salute you, friend, for your courage!
You nobly take up the hard yoke,
never complaining or losing hope,
you inspire me beyond measure.

Each time I call and hear your voice,
filled with joy or soberly somber.
I always know when the news is good
and I feel your pain when it is not.

The tears fall, you're often tired, and there
are days when you have no strength.
Still, you hide your feelings bravely
behind a smile and a sense of duty.

I'm sure you think about your kids,
loving and wanting the best for them,
wondering how their lives will be
if you're no longer able to care.

These grievous thoughts torment me,
as I ask God to lighten this cross.
I pray and hope He will listen closely,
to my prayer for your remission.

INCARCERATED *(Based on a true Story)*

Can this be happening to me? Imprisonment?
I'm living a nightmare! It is simply incredulous!
My freedoms can't be taken away, or can they?
And yet, here I am, in this hellhole, this jail.
When and how did such a violation occur?
I've done nothing wrong—I am innocent!!!

But still incredibly, here I am… isolated,
numbered, tagged, incarcerated in this cell.
What liar has chained me to this institution
where my liberties have been ravaged?
Housed here are the wicked and perverse,
not those I knew in my former quiet life.

If this is a prank I wonder when it will end.
I can't believe the intolerance of this dilemma.
I've seen movies of tragedies like this,
a travesty of justice unfurled because I had no defense.
No witnesses to proclaim my innocence.
No advocate to defend me in my hour of need.

Why God, why me?? What have I done to deserve this?
Where is justice as I weep for the loss of my freedom???
Have I no friend to believe me and take my side?
No benefactor or counselor to plead my case?
I will gratefully accept the crumbs of any compassion
and wait for an exit from this tyranny.

I am caught in a web of mistaken identity.
It's their word against mine… no proof either or…
My accusers have all the cards in their hands,
and I have nothing but feeble alibis to plead my case.
Truly, it is a compilation of lies and I pay the price.
Justice comes not—and the onslaught continues…

I'VE LOST MY POEM

(In Memory of Frans Minjeur, told to me by Leny)

"I've lost my Poem," my life, my love!
The song in my heart and soul is silent,
gone forever from the world we knew.
Our years together were once invincible.

Now, the loneliness engulfs me—
The sound of your voice echos at dawn.
The coffee we shared at the table and
"beschuitjes" rounds with butter and jam.

The walks to the little garden
where we planted living memories, and the
times with family gathered 'round the piano
filling the room with song, laughter and joy.

Yes, nighttime was peaceful and calm,
we were side by side for so long.
Now I lay in bed thinking of you often,
and how sad half of me is missing.

Aye, we had our share of troubles,
with health and mobility a strain.
But now life, one without the other,
is like not having a life at all.

And so, Frans, I miss you dearly,
my husband, friend, my love, my life.
One day, we will meet again in heaven,
the journey that will make us "home" again.

> *Recall it as often as you wish,*
> *A happy memory never wears out. Libbie Fudim*

PANDEMONIUM

I'm at a party with many people.
    I sit at the bar chatting with one,
sharing grief, sorrow, tragedy.
    I ponder what turmoil some come from.
What "sentences" we all have.
    Perchance, like dust in the wind.
Ironic as it seems, thoughts are alive with feelings—
    they live and breathe.

I feel compassion for this person.
    A life of struggle—a life just begun.
What dysfunctional, nay, tumultuous family
    brought this… all mixed up and apart.
Trying to fix what needs be mend…
    but no success in trying to make it right.
Advise to, "trust in God and pray a lot."
    What can one do other than that?

Sometimes it seems like it's out of our hands
    to help the distraught.
I am only a human—only one in the cacophony of many.
    I don't have all the answers.
How can we know how or where to guide
    such persons on their journeys.
I guess, just be there to listen and console.
    And God will intervene and do the rest.

THE CORN MAZE

The dried corn stalks wave in fall,
allowing the plow to make a path.
Acres of golden hair bend to the wind,
designing a maze like a game of chess.

Life is like the corn maze,
turning this way and that.
Getting lost and feeling alone,
longing to find the path home.

Every being must run the gauntlet.
No one escapes or finds it easy.
Life is full of twists and turns
And ne'er one can alter the course.

In the end, the way is poignant,
the spirit knows when the end is near.
Like homing pigeons with inner radar
telling us that the Farmer is ready.

Then the path is cleared and vision restored,
 all the trials and errors are left behind.
And a new, lush, fragrant way descends
bringing us home… checkmate.

THE EYES HAVE IT

For my friend, Dr. Jesse J. Cardellio, D.O.

It has been said, the eyes are the windows of the soul.
In their mirrors, one can perceive the entity of a person—
kindness, acceptance, anger, indifference, sadness, or love.

How wondrous the organ of vision—the miracle of sight!
And those who study and maintain their health, preventing disease
and blindness.

Unparalleled, Jesus gave the blind man back his sight.
But to be united with Him today, in the gift of knowledge,
the doctor can assist in sustaining this awesome mystery.

How great is your goodness and majesty, O Lord!
Thankfully, that humble men and women can aid in helping mankind
in Your works of mercy and healing!

THE LANGUOR OF THE DRINK

A human turns to drink to calm the savage beast,
impaled by the feeling of hopeless inadequacy.
Ah, but it salves the intelligence and sorrowful soul
from the pain of helplessness and woe,
and the vigor of youthful dreams dispelled.

The languor of feeling nothing—no pain or regret
(or so it seems!) a moment's peace of mind and solace,
tranquility of no thinking or planning or fixing.
No soul-searching or hopeless, endless trying
to make a difference where there is no power.

How does one climb from the depths of despair?
Right or wrong, human misery and suffering
can be imagined and understood because it is a sword
shared by all mortal men at one time or another.
In drink there are no boundaries—only imagined peace.

Is it a matter of loneliness and being unloved?
Or is it deception that no one cares or sympathizes?
How many people in the world experience isolation—
Troubles too many and friends too few, reclaiming
what's left of an ego in momentarily drowning to forget.

The irony of the drink is that it doesn't solve problems—
In the early light of morning, the beast returns
devouring what's left of one's self-esteem and dignity.
And the beast plunders on until the wretched body
has withered and destroyed its deceptive shell of propriety.

WHEN CHILDREN LEAVE HOME

(The Empty Nest Syndrome)

No one can prepare you for the day children leave.
            It's unexpected even though it's expected!
The insecurity of not being useful and needed…
            the agony of not being included.
No one could tell us how it would be,
            because no one knows this until it happens.

One by one, they seek their own lives
            and search for their hearts' desires.
We did the same, didn't we? Our parents let us go.
            Each generation does it similarly and yet…
when it happens, it is always unique
            and somewhat unsettling.

Now we are only memories to them of what was.
            Activities of many years, remembering
the joy of their chatter, laughter and song!
            A caring Mom and Dad who read stories, went camping,
baked cookies, played soccer, and made costumes,
            all in a dim past. Where did our lives go?

Somehow it reeks of unwelcomed change—
            Change followed by emptiness and loneliness.
Someone once quoted, "You give them roots,
            and then you let them have their wings."
It is wisdom, but it is nevertheless, sad.
            I suppose we will get over it—after we weep!

Life's Journeys
and U-turns

A SIBLING'S JOURNEY BACK IN TIME

We were not close as youngsters, my bro and I.
Perhaps different genders—I was oldest—
Different personalities, not a lot in common.
He went to trade school—I went to business college.
He went to Vietnam; I got married. Met at family events.
We lived separate lives—except for Mom's things.
He did outside chores. I did inside, doctors and bills.

Years went by—Mom needed more memory care.
Moved her to assisted living. Daily visits and help.
Mom fell and in an instant life forever changed for us.
Joe and I got closer because of circumstance.
Ultimately Mom died and we were together again.
A different, warmer relationship was established.
Just the two of us now—welcoming—endearing.

Remembering Mom, the good times and bad.
Recalling our youth without Dad, the ravages of the war.
Poverty, sickness, marriages, children and their problems.
And now it is our advancing ages and retirement.
We've changed a lot since our childhood 60 plus years ago.
Mellowed and experienced, we've lived all facets of life.
Enlightened we understand—our lives now a journey in time.

What one loves in childhood stays in the heart forever...
Mary Jo Putney

CULPABLE

We are all culpable… guilty of right or wrong…
but mostly omission.
We fail to do what is needed by overlooking
and pretending not to notice.
It doesn't matter if its relationships, work, home,
family, faith or politics.
Why are we negligible?
Are we ignorant of our duty?
No… We sit back, watch, and wait
for the other guy to act.
Then, and only then,
does need finally get our attention.
Really, most of life's compromises
are of procrastination.
Laziness is habit forming.

We allow ourselves to fall
into a mode of indifference.
Wake up, O foolish people!
Night comes and the lamp is out!
Do not expect that time will be there
for second chances and new beginnings.
Be responsible for living righteously…
And the journey begins now.

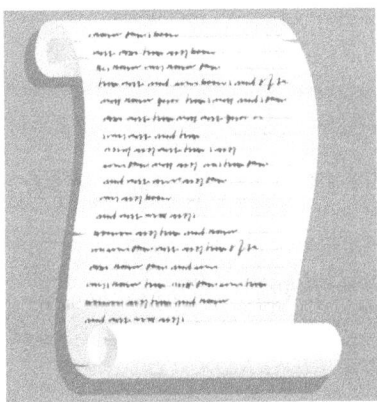

LIFE—AN ANCIENT SCROLL?

Is the existence of life simply an ancient scroll
created ages and ages ago, containing an infinite
amount of tasks one must complete?
The scribe eagerly awaits the start of life,
only to begin crossing off tasks, one by one.
O, how are we led to believe this dismal existence?
Life, I admit, happens betwixt these numerous tasks.
It slowly creeps upward through accomplishments
and challenges, like an acorn budding
through soil and rock.

The seedling is ever yearning—reaching
for the sun, as with any new life.
Similarly, we cannot choose where we are planted
or what the path upward will bring.
But we will always know, and count on, the
unimaginable beauty that awaits the sprouting bud.
For the seedling has worked past much soil and rock,
ensuring the strong foundation for a new life.

Copyright by Carel A. Minjeur II
(Used with permission)

LIFE IS A JOURNEY HOME

We are born… of billions of possibilities!
Think of the magnitude of genes and DNA.
Truly a wonder that you and I are here!

Human life… a most precious gift! Astounding!
Men and women, with God's help, procreate.
A hand in creation… God's plan for us to go on.

The miracle of the body and all it capabilities.
Contemplate its magnificence and glory.
Designed and made in the image of the Creator.

The allotted time for each of us—unknown.
And yet a purpose for each soul on the planet.
Divinity and destiny play a huge part in chance.

The grace to know God and return to Him is sublime.
We look to a Supreme Being greater than ourselves,
and glorify our Deity for this fragile existence.

Time is marked for everyone; we do not know the hour…
when He, the Master Builder, will call us to Himself
Thus, our life is truly plotted for the Journey Home.

    Life is the childhood of our immortality… Goethe

THE GREAT DIVIDE

The Great Divide begins with disagreement,

which leads to dissention,

which leads to alienation,

which leads to intolerance,

which leads to dislike,

which turns to hatefulness,

And ends with the Great Divide.

Leave the past to the mercy of God.
the future to the providence of God.
and the present to the love of God.

St. Augustine

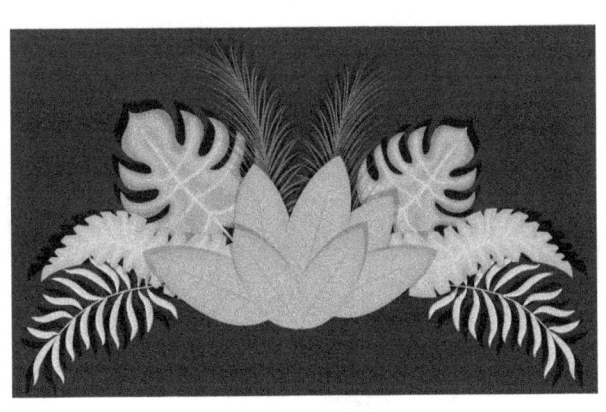

Love Conquers All

Francis and Hannah

A LOVE STORY *(For Francis and Hannah)*

A betrothal after many years knowing each other,
dreaming of futures, despite different majors in college,
living apart for what seemed like an eternity,
studying abroad and Skyping to visit one another.

Well, now the story comes to an end… really a beginning.
The wedding date is set and events will come to fruition
according to a timeline long since planned.
A joining of two souls and a blissful life in store.

The odyssey of a love story is that it never ends,
but evokes involvement, grows deeper, and lasts forever.
It doesn't move straight, but meanders through
the good times and bad—with trust and friendship.

And so our wishes for you both are lasting happiness,
the grace for God to enrich your lives with good things,
and fulfill your lives with joy and family.
Go with God and all our love forever.

Love, Mom and Dad

A MOMENT'S DESPAIR...

I know how it feels to be on the other side of love.
No longer is my champion my advocate.
Dismal are the wages of conflict that brought regret.
Caring has escaped and there is no way to drag it back.
The sculptor has sanded away the image of honor.
Kindness is chiseled to sharp arrowheads,
slaying self-esteem and leaving insecurity.
The particles of alabaster dust linger everywhere—

Egos-smitten, self-respect—debris on the floor.
What's left are mounds of clay—no likeness to what was,
ostracized and sent to oblivion like exploding asteroids.
Where love resided is now an empty shell—alas a tomb
that harbors hardened hearts and broken bodies.
Alas, the pedestal that rose to the sky is the rock of ages,
albeit a memory dim with the repetition of untruths.
Aye, we are enslaved to its awful damnation,
until forgiveness overtakes pride, and atonement reigns.

LOVE SMOTHERS DIFFERENCES

Marriage—a blend of two personalities.
Young love focuses on attraction in the beginning.
Children bring a life of busyness and joy.
Work and play wraps all in active happiness.
But in between, our idiosyncrasies interfere
at times with complete harmony and peace.
One's stratagems and peculiarities are visible
occasionally and stun or dampen the glow.
The snoring, the messes, occasional arguments,
inattentiveness, being unsupportive or secretive.
The partner generally steps back to regroup.
Another round to accept, or reject, and go on.

What is the cement that glues relationships?
On reflection, it is love that endures all things.
It is love that forgives, forgets and accepts
the imperfect spouses that we sometimes are.
It is love that goes deeper, beyond reality,
that subdues our selfish displays of snobbishness.
Tolerance, patience, and silence are forms of love,
and these too are part of the marital commitment…
for better or worse, richer or poorer… hence,
"Liefde overwinnen alles," Love conquers all.
Therein lies the truth and the answer…
Love is what smothers differences!

Mary and Carel's 25th Anniversary

DIVINE FORTUNE—25

Our "divine accident" turned into a "divine fortune,"
after 26 plus years of marriage and three sons!
How does anyone know what roads will lead to
happiness, success, fulfillment, cherished love,
faith, longevity and bliss?

We chose well, with blessings from above,
weathered storms, and put out brush fires
now and then, with forgiveness at the helm.
We managed it all amidst an endless sea of tasks
to be accomplished, work to be done,
support to be given, and sacrifices made.

Through it all, we were friends… and still are.
No matter what, loyalty and trust remain
when love is there.
God planted a flower just for me… it blooms every day,
and I know when time is no longer
we'll still be together.

The strongest evidence of love is sacrifice… John Eldredge

Carel and Mary's Anniversary Cruise

TAKEN FOR THE TAKING

The ocean waves wash o'er me
and the sun warms my weary soul.
The man fills my heart with song
and love's chalice is poured out.

I am taken for the taking.
No will or value do I own.
I am only what is beholden…
spirit, muscle, flesh and bone.

Mock courage is forsaken—
perhaps 'twas never known.
Good will has been replaced
by harbored dreams, oh so long.

THE MARRIAGE BLESSING OF CAREL AND MONICA

How many words have been written about love and marriage?!
    The world is full of verse on wedded bliss and blessings.
What new thing can be said about two people starting out?
    What wisdom has yet to be discovered about falling in love?

Jesus said it all… **Love one another as I have loved you.**
    And the Bible says, "In the beginning God made man and woman…"
The beginning and the end are encompassed in your vows.
    A life-long commitment to love and be loved and procreate.

How simple God made it; there is nothing magical or mystic
    Time… it is the way of the Trinity and of the Divinity of God.
Love will continue to grow, even unbeknown to the lover,
    as time cements the mortar and hardens the labors of the heart.

An edifice of pure delight and happiness is created day by day,
    as the sun rises and sets, and the tide ebbs and flows.
All rests in the hush of the Almighty and the peace of the night,
    when our souls and bodies are renewed by prayerful sleep.

Then a new day dawns and love and blessings begin anew,
    toiling and striving to work hard for this life and the next.
The continuous motion of time and communication to be cherished,
    is the ultimate **wonder of the gift and receipt** *in love and marriage.*

God's blessings, Carel and Monica, for a happy and holy wedded life.
With Love, Mom and Dad

Carel and Monica

Ann and Patrick

THE WEDDING BLESSING FOR PATRICK AND ANN

The Day Is At Hand—Two Hearts Are Now One.
　　　Patrick And Ann Are Wed. Let Us Rejoice!
Now Life Begins In Earnest And Living Your
　　　Sacred Vows A Lifelong Quest.

With Each Day That Passes, Love Grows Stronger.
　　　True Love Changes, But Never Slips Away.
Compromises, Listening And Sharing Help To Blend
　　　An Exemplary Life And Total Commitment.

Marriage—The Most Sanctified Role Of The Creator!
　　　One In Which The Beholden Are Co-Creators
And Architects In Continuing The Human Race
　　　A Privilege Only Parents Can Know!

Joys And Sorrows Will Accompany Your Journey,
　　　No One Escapes Those Sometimes Awful Roles,
But Hope In The Lord And Devout Prayers
　　　Will Bring You Safely Through Life's Troubles.

Bless You, Patrick And Ann, On This Day And In Your Life,
　　　That You Will Have All The Joy And Happiness
That God Wants All Of Us To Share In.
　　　Today Is The Day, The Lord Has Made
　　　Let Us Be Glad And Rejoice!

God bless you Patrick and Ann with a happy and holy wedded life!
Love, Mom & Dad

WHEN LOVE COMES

When love comes, sons suddenly turn away.
No more do they listen to your archaic wisdom.
They drift and succumb to be comforted—
benignly guided by their new-found friends.

What once made them saunter our way,
now transcends to other subtle powers.
Tenuously and surely, like moths to the flame,
love's finger is beckoning and affection beguiling.

Attracted now by shared times and places,
reaching out, other arms guide them to happiness.
No longer Mom or Dad answering their quest,
they depart and veer to uncertain destinies.

Walking hastily away more often now,
times have changed their needs, their wants.
Behold our sons are now their own men,
and life for us has changed forevermore.

*The best things you can give children, next to good
habits, are good memories... Sydney J. Harris*

Francis, Hannah, Patrick, Ann, Carel, and Monica

Precious Moments

*There are no seven wonders of
the world in the eyes of a child.
There are seven million…*

Walt Streightiff

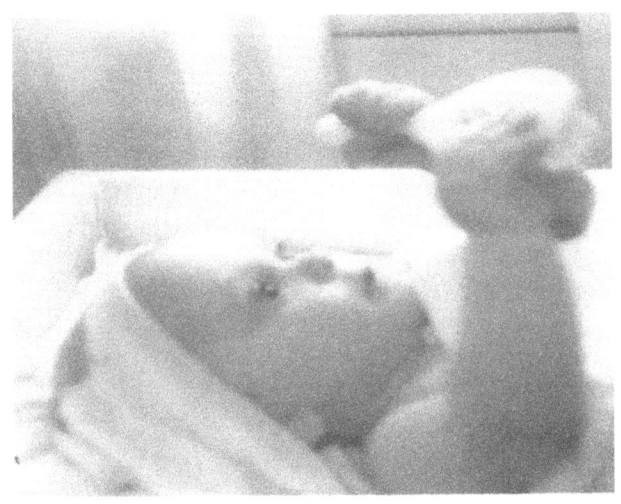

THE MIRACLE

In the grey half-shadows

of a cold, wintry dawn,

I look upon the face of

my sleeping babe,

nestled in my arms

and know God is with us

He sends His love in a

miracle such as this.

LIFE IS BUT A BREATH

Life is but a breath like mist rising on a cold dawn.
*   The minute we are born with a tap on the feet,*
the breath we take sustains us for a time allotted.

Not a hint of how long that is will be known;
*   Only the Creator knows for certain.*
So much to accomplish and learn.

Ask an elderly person you see how fast time flies!
*   Ask the young person who gobbles up the day.*
Witness, all, how time is never enough.

A life is given—a gift to fill with activity and virtue.
*   Every life precious—equally full, and equally busy.*
Long or short, no matter, projects and things are left undone.

The scope of living is an awesome and noble entity,
*   bringing satisfaction and fulfillment to an apex.*
Then winding down to acceptance that all is completed.

Finality—the time when the last inhalation brings peace
*   and anticipation that another breath will take us home—*
home to an everlasting heartbeat living forever in Him.

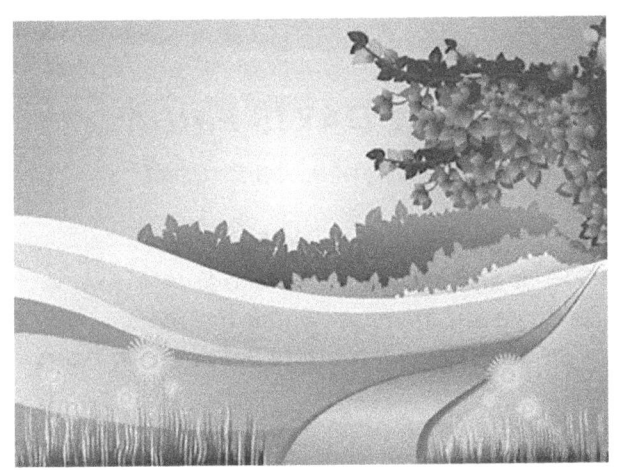

PAT'S SOLILOQUY

My mind starts to wander and I feel like

a row in an endless field of grass…. .

EVERY DAY IS FRIDAY

(Memoirs of husband, Carel)

Ah, retirement… glorious freedom!
 Rest and relaxation—the ultimate goal.
Sleep or eat anytime, watch the birds,
 sit on the patio, feet up, with beer in hand,

But as the week ends, Friday hits a chord.
 When working, that day was special.
Now every day is "Friday" to do as I please.
 The wonder of it is fascinating.

No boss to give me instructions,
 or rushing to drive to and from work.
No answering phones or hurrying
 to get a report done or a part made.

I never realized how great it would be!
 I wake up full of enthusiasm.
What should we do for fun today, Hon???
 I have a thousand things to try.

I mow the grass, fix things, cut the hedges—
 It doesn't matter—it's all exciting.
I thank the Lord for this new life,
 with all the hustle and bustle and joy!

FAREWELL LITTLE BIRD

So many years have gone by!
How quickly the time went—
almost twenty-four to be exact.

Now my little bird flies northwest,
to an abode of his own.
In sudden abandonment,
all that took place in a lifetime
appears in my mind's eye.

Memories—laughter and tears,
growing and sharing the daily routine.
All coming to an end with the
beginning of a new tomorrow.

Am I ready? No!
Is anyone ever ready? No!
But such is life as each bird
seeks a new way for itself.

God's wisdom. God's plan.
Have a safe journey, Patrick.
Go with God and all our love.
Don't forget to fly home now and then.

Love, Mom and Dad 8-18-09

REVELATIONS OF THE MIND

*All the thoughts in my head
cannot reveal who I am,
for I don't really know.*

*Who is this creature who has
so many chasms of discrepancy?
Age only widens the gap of clarity.*

*I am a blend of so many ideas
feelings, knowledge and… ignorance.
Lord, who am I?*

*I am a grain of sand in a landscape
populated with a magnitude of difference!
Like the billions of stars in the universe.*

*To contemplate all the opinions all of us have
since time began is incomprehensible!
I can't ponder the ecstasy, or the agony, of thinking!*

HAPPY ST. PATRICK'S DAY

We'll raise a glass or two,
And celebrate with you.

We'll sing Irish songs
And dance the whole night long.

Good times we'll have today
For tomorrow we will pay,

So bonny lads and lasses
Drink ye a few glasses

And smile all the while
With your friends from the Isle

For today everyone is Irish!

THE COTTAGE

The cottage tucked away in a forest of trees…
pines and oaks abounding,
housing youthful dreams and laughter,
activities and fun galore.

All vanished now years later—
the sons grown and gone.
Echoes and traces of children's games and toys
whisper in the silence—ghosts of memories past.
Their images linger in the dim light as we
listen for their voices fading into the night.

Where did those days go?
Fleeting they went into a black hole of time,
rushing and passing us while we blindly
lived on and on… and tomorrow,
sadly, came and went.

The Beauty of the Earth
and the Majesty of God

BEAUTY IN CHAOS

Visit, weary spirit, the sleepy forest…
See pines bending o'er wispy ferns while
gentle breezes pull ivy over marred paths.
Fronds and mosses creep over scented
Trumpet Vines and Lilies of the Valley.
All vegetation meanders over toppled
deadwoods—once majestic maples and oaks,
crisscrossing in chaotic beauty.

See Lady slippers and Pussytoes
dance with Jack in the Pulpits,
and Fairy Lanterns lighten the gloom.
Thimble heads of Morel mushrooms burst
straining to the dismal light.
Frogs seeking mates croak in puddles
and trilogies of birds chirp in treetops.
Such magnificent plunder amid random aesthetics
drawn in the resplendence of nature.

No camera or artist's canvas can capture the glory
 of quiet ramblings in an untouched environment,
ablaze with color and unseen activity askew.
The sanctity of God's creation is really here.
And time stands still in joyful tranquility.
The inhabitants and music in this glade beckon,
renewing the spirit and man's longing for solitude.

DOES GOD VISIT THE EARTH

*Does God sit in the mountains and hills
     of the world He made,
Scanning the sunrise on the horizon
     cutting through gourds in the mist?
Does He smell the pines and feel the cold
     dewy dampness of daybreak?
Imagine His presence—His Being
     just knowing he is Author of all!*

*Does He dwell among His creatures in the
     wondrous earth He fashioned?
Does He listen to bird song and the cries
     and laughter of His people?
Does He reflect upon our past and future
     plights on this planet?
And does He plan our days and nights—
     the pawns in His game of life?*

continued

Lo and behold, the blueprint for life on earth
is majestic wonderment!
But does our Creator partake of the splendor
and the wonder of it all!
What of the oceans and rippling brooks—
water that sustains the living.
Does He "dream" under starry nights designing
more ways to beautify the universe?

Ah, peace and stillness of forests at sunset—
earth at rest except the nocturnal.
How can a simple brain the size of an ant realize
the grandeur and mind of God?
Wouldn't it be sensible that He enjoy His works
and glance at it all—very pleased,
like an artist critiquing his paintings,
while the world acclaims the greatness.

THE MAGNIFICENT EARTH *(From Las Vegas to Detroit)*

The wings of our plane cut through the grey mist,
     over Kansas now—so the pilot says.
Turbulence makes the plane vibrate and shake.
     I can only think how much faith men
put into mechanical things. After all, what's holding us up
     35,000 feet above the earth?
Only an engine, some aluminum strips,
     and frames of the same composition.

Peering through the oval windows,
     a miniscule version of life appears.
But seeing the world from above as God made it
     is awesome in all its wonder and glory.
We cut through spiking clouds
     building high-rise towers of misshaped cotton.
Rivers below are like silver ribbons cutting through
     a monstrous apron of arid limestone.
The Grand Canyon looms ahead—
     yawning and gaping like a multitude of anthills.

continued

Surely in a wisp of fast-forward, a continent jogs by
       as we inch closer to our destination.
Mile after mile, we race into Eastern Standard Time,
       seeing the sun disappear in ever darkening skies.
The stars appear like fireflies above and below
       the sporadic cities' lights twinkle softly.
The beauty of it all makes reflections on life
       come to the forefront of my mind.

Here we are, closer to God than ever.
       I think of a friend who was called from life today,
who has now escaped all her troubles and pain.
       I dwell on this thought and think,
"Did she pass me by enroute to her new destiny?"
       What of all the other spirits this day who
went the same way? Do they meander at the same
       altitudes as our metallic, plastic flying bird?

I realize I am relatively insignificant in the great scheme
       of all that has been and is yet to be.
I am a puff of wind in the sea of air, dark now,
       as we head east toward home.
The comfort of dusk is day's end—perhaps for some—
       life's end. Similar the two—so similar.
I'm at peace thanking my Father for the gifts
       of man's ingenuity and a safe flight.

Yes, I guess I trust, like all the others,
       that all is well—the Captain is at the helm.
The mechanics did their jobs well,
       and flight attendants routinely cared for guests.
The flight of this airbus is on time
       and will end as planned on schedule.
Thanks be to God for His great gift--
       the brilliance and magnificence of earth.

OF DUSK

The fading shadows of daylight,
        emulating a transition from life to death.
The foreboding hour of doom and abandonment
        until darkness lays a warm blanket o'er the earth.

The night descends and brings peace to one's soul
        following the restlessness of sunset.
Unsettling is the longing for sleep and security
        which comes as God bids "good night" to His children.

I ask, "Will I live to see another day?"
        "Will I have another chance to begin anew?"
I envision night wrapped in the arms of God
        and peace restoring my weary spirit.

O, my ever wanton desire to be with the Father!
        To simply be comforted and reassured,
knowing that I am truly loved and worthy,
        until dawn blooms with new hope for atonement.

The Sorrows of the Heart

BROKEN

I am broken now… .
> *Your words have cut me through.*
I can't rise to the occasion—
> *My flesh has turned to jelly.*

Speech has betrayed me ---
> *Thoughts of rebuttal escape.*
Words no longer make sense
> *The irony of dilemma.*

What's left but to bare
> *all the bitterness in one's heart.*
Of being wrong and ignored
> *because I loved too much.*

GHOST WRITER

I am truly transparent—not knowing myself.
I breathe, I eat, I sleep, I think, I am…
But who am I? Really?
Sometimes I feel like putty…
to be sculpted into something substantial.

Other times, I feel like water that
pours out of the mold to mingle with the sea.
Have I a cliché or a tangible thought
to give the world to insure my place?

Or is it just garble that spews out of my mouth,
like marshmallows and sand that serve no one.
Have I ever done a good thing that will be
worth remembering or otherwise something
that can be spoken of in ages to come.

Is it that important?? Or am I a phantom like
the willows in the windswept cliffs of oblivion?
My destiny—my legacy—my emptiness
is all there is of me—the ghost writer.

DRIFTWOOD

I am driftwood floating on the ocean waves,
waterlogged and shriveled waiting for the neap tide
that will send me ashore to find my final resting place.
I long to be marooned in sand, windswept and abandoned
so my sorrows will no longer afflict me.

I am aged like the cedar that has been tempest tossed
and battered on the surf for ages it seems,
gathering moss and seaweed, being plucked by the
puckered lips of fish searching for a meal.

What once was joy, has become unbearable
and now intolerable. I think back to the early days
when tides came in and life flowed in perfect rhythm.
Avast! It's ripped out to sea by undercurrents that I did
not foresee—did not expect—did not dream of.

Where once sailed my sloop on calm ripples of glass
and the jib filled with fragrant breezes,
now finds the vessel asunder, bereft of nobility
and lonely as the blackest night.

continued

Alas! The storms and swells have plied my fate
and I flounder in the tempest like a cork
bobbing on a briny sea of loneliness.
Will dawn come and my hope be restored?
The silence only hisses back the word "Never."

For a lifetime came and went its way—only once
do we come this way. I'll not have the time again
to find the answer; but perhaps when I'm reincarnated…
in the womb of eternity—to the Maker who beckons.

EMPTY ECHOES

Where has "my career" gone?
When did "the kids" leave?
You know—the busyness of family
and their constant demands.
The never-ending days of questions,
homework, cleaning, and cooking.

They no longer need me to kiss their fingers
and wipe away their tears, bandaging
their cuts and scrapes and bruised egos.
No more requests to push their sleds
down the snow-covered backyard hills,
and no more dandelion bouquets in summer,
given with smiles and twinkling eyes.

No more noisy chatter and booster seats
at restaurants with placemat menus,
and nighttime stories on my lap before bed.
They have disappeared into oblivion—adulthood—
leaving their little love letters and drawings
from tender hearts—tucked away in my diary.

Now, the yellowed pages are what I leaf through,
flashbacks recalling their adoration and trust.
Memories of little hands that once held mine,
and hugs around my neck I can still feel.
And mostly missing the echo of my name—
The sweetest name of all—"Mom."

SHALOM... PEACE

I search for peace in the catacombs of life…
trudging through webs of intolerance and deception.
I harbor thoughts of pride and superiority, but
what have I done to atone for my salvation?
At daybreak the choices begin opting for goodness.
Alas, I chastise myself for omissions and outright faults!
How will I ever reach the perfection I seek?
The labyrinth of comforting old ways drag me down
until I'm drowning in disgusting self-pity.
Knowledge tells me I have no reason to despair—
I am so blessed by our Creator with His gifts!

But then, what am I lacking to be happy?
Uncertain, I try yet another path
to righteousness, and most of all, love.
The hope returns daily but the virtue eludes me,
and unwelcomed self-centeredness prevails.
I accuse myself of wretched complacency.
Lord, forgive my frailty in these attempts!
I seek to be your follower but I fall short of my goal.
Please grant me the grace to keep trying
until I can see your face on the last day.
Then will I know triumph, and… peace.

SHARDS OF CONVICTION

The windowpanes of morals have long
     ago turned to shards,
relinquishing all that once was believed.
In time, all that one knows and trusts and lives
crumbles like glass in the wake of time.
The steadfastness of faith turns to dust with
each new generation.

Ethics and honor fade into the oblivion of indifference.
Where did all the convictions go?
The Ten Commandments? Integrity?
Gone forever is righteousness and wisdom
succumbing to insensitivity and advanced age.
Enter the existing era of now… and hold one's breath…

SIGNS OF DISPARITY

What once I could foresee no longer exists.
I used to have everything figured out pretty much.
Now life once certain is disparaging at best.
Dismal and dreary are future tidings I think,
left as crumbs from the banquet table.

Weariness shows in the sag of my walk,
and tear-stained eyes weep to the morrow.
News and foretelling of what's to come,
weighs down my spirit and frame.
All seems lost but to turn to an awesome God.
Since now is the twilight—the years gone by.

Only hope and a promise abounds when life is o'er,
a paradise for the searching soul awaits.
Longing turns to need and then desperation
and once more anticipation awakens the will,
as time marches on to the drumline…

Love guarantees immortality by our Christ,
and peace is not in earthly dimensions.
We must weather it well for we will
experience the demise of passions one day,
trading them for happiness and tranquility,
in the warm, embracing arms of God.

SUBTLE BURDENS

Did you know parents are burdens now?
They no longer have youth or pizzazz
to make it in the world of young adults.

Embarrassing, not cool, and not savvy,
we interrupt the swing of things,
like ham sandwiches taken to a banquet.

We're not spry, fun or entertaining.
We're far from understanding slang,
and forget asking for computer help!

Times have changed since our youth…
parental wisdom was sought and welcomed.
Respect and joy was evident in life's activities.

Barren now, the ideas of youth—beware,
lo, the day will come to rue insensitivity and
rethink the philosophies of Mom and Dad.

What once made family is cast aside,
craters of indifference and selfishness loom,
growing like weeds in cracked sidewalks.

Only one thing is certain—time marches on.
What was today will also be tomorrow's fare.
Progeny: what goes 'round will come 'round.

WILL THEY PUT FLOWERS ON MY GRAVE

I walk alone through the cemetery,
first to stand o'er the grave of my oldest son,
pulling the weeds around his stone,
squaring it off to see the engravings.

The perennials have come up,
color and greens spiking at his head.
I kneel and pray, "I miss you, son."
"Why?" I ask one more time.

I drift from there to other sites…
uncles, aunts, Mom's, a family's haven,
peaceful, calm, thinking all the while,
will anyone put flowers on my grave?

I yearn to see each loving face again,
standing there, missing them, shedding tears,
silently conversing with them as if they lived,
telling them my detailed events and concerns.
Then, I wonder why it's always too late,
when the person you love is gone forever.
The lesson is to speak what's in the heart
while we have the chance before it's lost.

Why can't we know now what matters most:
It's family! Tell them how much you love them.
Say it every day—think it every moment, and
live like every day could be your last together.

WORTH

What is worth, you know, self-esteem?
Something substantial… I guess.
What makes one significant,
important or phenomenal?

Is it connections? Or knowledge?
Is it education or opportunity?
Is it a prestigious job or occupation?
How about life experience?

Is it more interesting or dangerous?
Is it entertaining or amusing?
Is it expounding on religious or political beliefs?
Is it rhetoric or having more to say?

I seem to have none of these…
What then is worth? Substance?
Maybe it won't materialize
for me in this lifetime… but then

there's always another time and place
where class won't matter and
other's opinions won't count!

Tragedies

DEMENTIA

Amidst the sinking feelings of strife
     and endless decisions,
The mind grows closed with glue…
     Fractured, broken neurons shut down
even with the very best of intellect and joy.

Alas, memory is compromised and
     welfares obleaked.
What say those who misunderstand the victim?
     Try to remember and be happy??
What is left of a person once known,
     when dementia takes over and
the identity vacates?

DIFFERENT GENERATIONS

What makes old age intolerable?
The anguish of a child's insolence?
Awful remarks that pierce one's heart?
How can it be? I've never hated my flesh.

Yet, caustic statements afflict like a mallet,
and comments brand a heart full of love.
Words reverberate in hallowed crypts forever.
Forgive? Aye. Forget? Perhaps in time.

Flesh of my flesh, and bone of my bone,
miraculously my own… and yet…
the pillars do not meet—they are separate.
In truth, humans will never comprehend

the life of the other no matter the time.
Each individual enters a new dimension
that can never be touched by another.
Similarities exist, but no two are alike,

for time warp and existence are severed—
no pleading or explaining will change
the fact that each generation is of its own kind.
And God is the Creator of all the difference.

I KNOW I DON'T KNOW

(Ramblings of Mom with Alzheimer's)

I wasn't always like this…
> *trapped in a mind that doesn't remember…*
I really try hard not to forget,
> *but somehow my thoughts escape.*
I know I don't know anymore,
> *and I think people rob my things,*
drink my beer, take my clothes
> *and come into my house at night.*
When are you going on vacation?

I get frustrated and angry at myself!
> *It's like living in a thick fog—*
the mist blowing everywhere,
> *like cobwebs in my brain.*
I haven't eaten all day! I don't remember
> *many names—not even my cats.*
Did I always have two?
> *I haven't had a beer in three weeks!*
When are you going on vacation?

What day is it today?—oh,
> *I thought it was Sunday.*
Are the boys getting married yet?
> *Will you be glad when they do?*
Darn! I always miss my dinner. Sometimes
> *I'm lucid and suspect I don't recall things.*
And it really scares me to think I can't remember.
When are you going on vacation?

continued

I live in a shell—a tomb—and sometimes wish
        God would call me home.
I do remember early years square dancing and
        singing with the Sweet Adelines,
happy trips to Turtle Soup Inn for boombas and pizza.
        Then like quicksand, my memory fades,
and I'm back in my chair not knowing
        I remembered for a while.
When are you going on vacation?

It can be a blessing, though, when loneliness comes;
        thinking about my mom always makes me smile.
I remember my 10 older brothers and sister.
        I haven't heard from them in a while.
Are they still alive? I know Jesus and the Ten
        Commandments, and one day I'll be in heaven.
But I forget if I went to church today,
        or where I put my prayer book or rosary.
When are you going on vacation?

My children come and I know them… but my grandkids'
        faces change and I don't recognize them.
I hope they understand and have compassion, for one
        day we all have a cross that needs bearing.
I'm sorry if I annoyed or offended anyone
        with my musings and repetitive questions.
When are you going on vacation?

I supposed I asked you that quite a few times,
        but I have nothing else to ask that I remember.
Just love me as I am, be patient, and help me do what's
        left of my time the right way.
I've had a good life, and it won't be too long now.
        I'll miss you. All my love, Mom

(Mary died on January 12, 2010.
She knows everything now…)

Mom, Francis, Paul, Patrick, Mary Carel II, Carel

THANKSGIVING WITH MOM

*Our family picture with Mom sits on the mantel…
the last Thanksgiving together before she passed.
Who knew then in six weeks she would be gone.
The "last supper" with children, grandkids, and brother.*

*Even then, she was already in the first throes of death.
A slip and fall began a series of unsettling findings.
Destiny played its part wooing the life from her
while we tried desperately to change the outcome.*

*Mom knew. She was ready to leave us for heaven.
Tired of pretending to be happy, and longing for the days
when her siblings and friends would smile, sing along, and
dance to the "Lawrence Welk Show," she succumbed.*

*Family. Heart. Where would we be without them?
Nothing in life is more important than familial love.
All the treasures and possessions in the world
cannot compare to the persons who care about you.*

*And yet, when the hour comes to leave, it is accepted.
There are no ties that can bind—not even family.
Love will be there forever, but the longing for God is
greater than life itself—we all will follow in time.*

THE BIRTHDAY I DIDN'T WANT TO REMEMBER

It's only been a few hours ago…
My mom struggling for every breath.
I knew the end was soon but it was so hard
watching her fade away from a life she loved.
My birthday was drawing ever so close.
The week before I told my family
she would die on the anniversary of my birth.
No one believed I could be so negative, especially
with such a positive outcome from her surgery.

Jan. 11, 11 PM—the nurse said it wouldn't be tonight, so
we left with the thought we'd see her in the morning.
At 5 AM, my birthday, we received "the call."
It was over. Mom went to heaven and I wasn't at her side.
Guiltily thinking I could have been there, I burst into tears.
I thought how horrible I would always remember
this terrible event every time I had a birthday.

Then a little consoling voice spoke to me saying,
"I am entering my eternal life, the day I gave you life!"
Immediately I realized this was a very comforting thought.
I believed then Mom spoke to me and gave me solace.
Death should not be unhappy—it is a celebration of new life!
Now I will always remember Mom with love and a smile,
And think of the birthday I didn't want to remember.

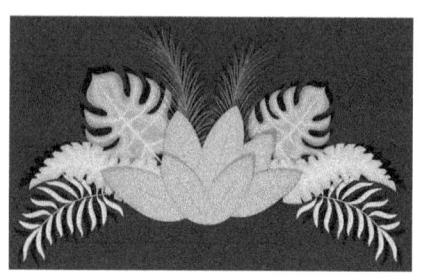

To every thing there
is a season…
a time to be born
and a time to die…

Ecclesiastes

We Live by Faith

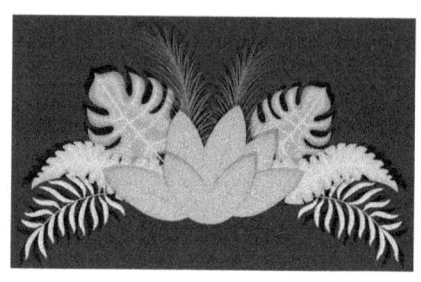

What is Charity?

It's silence when your

words would hurt.

Dolly Nazareno

BRING US BACK O LORD!

Bring us back, O Lord, from the precipice!
We are wandering away from simpler times—
times of security, wonder, trust, faith and joy.

Truth has been replaced by clever deceit.
Hopeful youth has turned into confused old age.
Floundering we look for the righteous path.

Burdened and heavy, we plow through days
of depression, guilt, fear, and boredom.
Where is your holy light to show us the way?

Beguiled, we are pulled in too many directions.
We are torn between good and not so good.
We have become desensitized and lazy.

There are so many orators and prophets!
Who can we trust; who can we believe?
Even seemingly holy men can be corrupt and evil.

Lord, save us from our prideful, foolish selves!!
Guide us through this dense fog of lies.
We long for your loving face; we long for You.

ETERNITY BEGINS NOW

I am dying… a little bit every day…
    seconds closer to the end.
Not of a disease, but still of
    a designated end time,
not of my choosing—
    or knowing when or how actually.
But it is there—for each and
    every human on the planet.
On days of intolerance,
    I'm ready to give it up sooner
other days I don't want to leave
    what I've left undone.
Which one of these options
    will win in the end?
Will it be attitude that brings longevity
    or good genes I inherited?
Or will it be some agonizing and
    long-suffering misfortune?

continued

I am saddened and troubled
        by the years that passed,
when I think I haven't measured up
        to what I thought I wanted to be.
Who will judge that? Who will care?
        My offspring or those who knew me?
I think not—since they will be reflecting
        upon the same issues as I,
analyzing themselves like I do now,
        searching for worth,
wanting to leave a mark on the earth
        that recognizes existence.
Isn't that what each being wants
        to leave behind—a legacy?
I'm not sure what should be done,
        said or unsaid to this end…

It's pointless to philosophize over
        thoughts about life… and death.
when we have no knowledge of either.
        old age and experience don't count.
The more years, the less wisdom we have
        since there are more reasons to fail.
Daily there are more choices to
        fathom with no conclusions
and no ultimatums to make—
        only rapid changes that fill each day.
And so, obscurely, we dwindle into
        a world that awaits our musings,
to begin anew the process of acquiring
        definition, dignity, and esteem,
justly and lovingly in the finale
        from the Father of all creation.

HOPE

Hope for joy comes with the sun's rays today,
     No room for despair—there's always a way,
You'll lose sadness, and weeping too, if you
     first shake off the old and bring in the new!
So, open your heart, be happy instead,
     let woes dry up when you get out of bed.
Nothing is gained by your tears and a huff,
     Instead, be delightful and bring on a bluff!

     He that is of a merry heart hath a continual feast.
                Proverbs…15:15

LAMENTATIONS

(Prayer in time of distress…)

Lord, I cry out to you with an awful vengeance!
I can no longer hide my feelings of despondence.
In all things I have failed and have come to a dead end.
My sanity, and even my salvation, do I question.
It seems the piety of my youth has left me confused,
and my faith collapsed like a building in an earthquake.
Where is my former strength and conviction, O God?
And my fortitude and stamina which once sustained me?

I was always certain of outcomes if I trusted in you.
Now my soul is enveloped in an impenetrable darkness.
Will I ever climb out of this fathomless, abysmal pit?
How I long to hear you and feel your hand on my shoulder,
comforting me like I comforted my children!
Now I raise my eyes heavenward to you with my pleas,
hoping these trials and tribulations will be lifted.

Do not forsake me, O Lord, for I am desperately alone;
vulnerable to many adversaries who convict me;
who try to destroy my very being with indifference.
I need you, my God, to sustain me on this difficult journey.
Join my agonies to yours in reparation for my indiscretions,
and assist me to endure whatever is your will.
I humbly ask this through Jesus Christ, my Lord and Savior.

MARY, LADY OF THE SALVATION ARMY

There she is… top shelf in the
      bric-a-brac isle.
White plaster, poor man's
      alabaster,
Eyes to heaven, hands upheld,
      one broken.
Beautiful form and stance—lovely.

Well, I guess I could fix the hand
      and shape it like the other.
Fifty cents. Hmm, a bargain.
      She calls to me—I can fix this

Perfect for my centerpiece at the weekly
      rosary I lead at the nursing home.
I bring her home and set her on the table.
      Get out newspaper and plaster of Paris.

Mix up the paste and begin a simple
      masterpiece of making another hand.
Lo and behold, it is fixed satisfactorily.
      I am very proud of my attempt.

continued

I bring her to the next session and she is well
　　　received. A few more times and then…
I open up the bag in which she's carried
　　　and, oh my! She is broken in many pieces!

O No! Is it worth my time to fix her?
　　　To put her together with so many bits?
Or should I find a new Virgin to fix our gaze upon?
　　　She keeps calling, calling me…

Well, I'll give it a try once more.
　　　I bring out the plaster of Paris again
and arrange the pieces to form the crown
　　　of her head and fill in the rest with paste.

Many hours go by and I still work
　　　on my lovely Virgin Mary.
It is finally put together, but…
　　　now there are lots of ridges to sand.

I decide to paint the statue blue, white, and flesh.
　　　Another day, until this is dry.
I timidly begin with her face and hands.
　　　So far so good—next the blue cape.

Stop for a day 'til this much dries.
　　　Begin again with hair and veil and face.
Now for the finale—a touch of silver in the folds.
　　　Done at last, she looks very nice indeed.

I stand back and look lovingly at my Lady
　　　from the Salvation Army.
I know she's smiling at me and is very pleased.
　　　I whisper, "I love you. Pray for us, Mary."

MY GOD IN THE SHOWER

Every night I am embraced by my God in the shower.
The cares and events of the day are gently washed away.
God comforts me as the water finely sprays on my uplifted face.
As I say His name, I begin to pray.

Thank you, Lord, for the gift of this day.
Pardon me if I did not use it to do your will.
Help me forgive those who have marred my path.
Bring me peace to know I've done my best.

Bless all those who are far away from home.
Comfort the sick and the dying and mostly the poor.
Help me to understand how to be more patient and tolerant.
I ask these as I stand before You in my humble nakedness. Amen.

PSALM OF SUBMISSION

Lord, what would you have me do? Please I am listening…
In the quiet hours of this day,
I am trying to put my life in order.
The chaos is what makes me so unsettled.
There is so much unrest in my soul.

I am ever in error—I am like the ashes that blow
      and scatter in the wind.
They spread me over the universe
      never to be heard from again.
I have endured much, and I have also learned much.
I know that if you are with me, I'll never walk alone.

I resign myself to whatever fate you have in store for me.
I am weary of planning, fearing, hoping,
      and the demands of all!
I'm finally the clay you need to mold me
      into whatever vessel you choose.
I no longer live for myself but in you.

Holy Spirit, I only ask that you guide me
      in making good decisions.
Help me overcome my fear of an uncertain future as old
      age approaches.
Grant me the grace to endure all misfortunes,
      disappointments, illness, and personal slights.
Let me be as you will, and love me as I am,
      for without you I am nothing.

THE INNOCUOUS COMPROMISING OF OUR VALUES

O God, I accuse myself of compromising
        values I no longer enforce.
I have become desensitized and watch
        as those I love turn their backs
on the righteousness of living your laws.
        I accuse myself of weakness.
How can this have happened?
        Slowly, innocuously, it crept into our daily life.

I am not the strict parent I was and find
        myself sandwiched in a wedge,
denying all that I have been taught
        and valued as good and righteous.
My parents raised me to be pious,
        do good deeds, repent, and pray.
We spent many hours in church
        attending Mass and receiving Eucharist.

Now I feel so far from the holiness
        I claimed as an innocent youth.
What did I do to fail myself and my family?
        I know less now than I did at age 12!
I felt closer to God then in the dark alcoves
        of the church I used to attend.
I was inspired by good books and now
        I wrestle with decisions of what I allow.

continued

Are the Ten Commandments still in existence
        for the youth of today?
What I always thought was honorable
        is no longer important or true it seems.
Nothing is the same as it was in my youth.
        It is very confusing and compromising,
and I cry for the lack of those values,
        calmness and structure today.

There are too many choices now...
        letting things go, pretending not to notice.
I do not interfere and say what I really think
        about the improprieties I witness.
God, forgive me my ignorance, my ineffectiveness
        and lack of fortitude.
The heartbreak is it will take years to effect change—
        perhaps by then it will be too late.

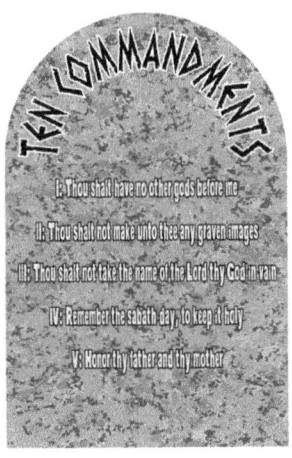

WHERE ARE YOU GOD?

In the vastness of the earth and sky, I look for you, my God.
In my loved ones, I search for your goodness and strength.
I am filled with anxiety, doubt, and fear—never did I think,
I would ever face these terrible demons of loss.

Separation is upon me—I have no peace—I have no hope.
All that I have ever dreamed of has turned to ash.
My world is emptying itself as if I betrayed it somehow.
I look for comfort and find overwhelming frustration.

No words of endearment—nor acts of sympathy—only dictates!
Has everyone gone mad? Is there not a conscientious soul left?
My heart is heavy with rejection, elusiveness, and put downs.
I think, how will I get through today, tomorrow, and life itself.

Unity has been replaced with extensions, caring has vanished.
Indifference permeates conversations and get-togethers.
Values are discarded and love seems to have disappeared.
I ask, where are you God? Have you abandoned us too?

Nothing is as it was—happiness and sharing—loving and caring.
Apathy has taken a stronghold and affection discarded.
Hopefully time will bring back the genuine togetherness of
family—the cement that brings peace and harmony to all.

The years teach much which the days never know...
Ralph Waldo Emerson

THE GRACE TO RETURN

I am thankful, Lord, for your grace—
the grace to return to the righteous path.
The dark night of my soul
comes and goes like smoke.
Yet you come for me again and again.

O how I long for your presence always!
Turn not your face from me.
Abide in me and I will welcome your grace.
Pursue me until I come home
where love is ever present and comforting.

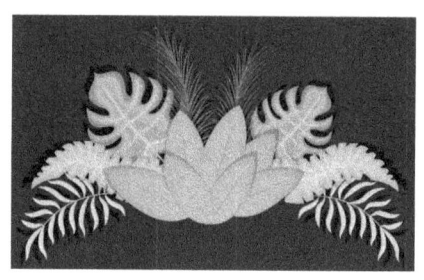

Pax et bonum…
Peace and every blessing…

St. Francis of Assisi

The Rescue of Sammy

Sammy at Age 2

Sammy age 4

Sammy at Age 7

Sammy age 10

THE RESCUE OF SAMMY

This is a true story about Sammy, a tiny, black, stray kitten who lived in a neighborhood in Detroit, Michigan. He appeared one day at my mother's doorstep, hungry and homeless, and being the kind-hearted person she was, began feeding him every day. She already had two cats of her own and couldn't take him in, but he didn't seem to mind his circumstances.

Little Sammy was all fur that first spring and would sit trembling in the cool mornings under mom's old car which was parked in the driveway. He was completely black and had fluffy fur which made him look twice his size, and his huge eyes were a beautiful yellow green. But his most significant feature was a "meow" that was startlingly loud for a cat of his small size.

Well, this kitten chased the mice and meandered down the street day and night. I felt bad that he didn't have a home and someone to love and care for him since he seemed to have a good disposition and was quite intelligent. As it was, though, the situation seemed okay. He was at least being fed and had shelter in a variety of places so I didn't worry. That all changed, however, when winter arrived with the cold and snow.

Somehow, between the other benevolent neighbors and my mom, Sammy survived the first winter of his life and made it to spring. By this time, Sammy was very street-wise and stealthy. He would stay out of your reach, but would come and take food left outside when everyone disappeared. He was wary of people and took care of himself against other cats, dogs, and some other critters that roamed the neighborhood. He was a tomcat and a survivor none the less.

When I saw him again the following spring in his usual spot at the back door, he was a full grown cat. I was surprised to see him, but there he was, expectantly pleading for a meal. He was a little shy, but still friendly.

The summer months passed and Sammy was ruffled and dirty and he had his share of fleas and ear mites. I still believed he would have made someone a beautiful pet, but now I couldn't be sure if he would even adjust to living with a family since he had become what I would call feral.

By November another winter was upon us and Mom's health took a turn for the worse requiring us to find different living arrangements for her. We moved her and her pets to an assisted living facility where she had daily care. I was quite preoccupied with this dilemma and didn't think about our daily visitor or what would happen to him.

In the meantime, I was getting her house ready to sell and Sammy would come up, as usual, to the side door for food. I kept feeding him because that's what mom would have done. I never knew where he went after he finished his meals and just assumed he found a place where he could hide and rest.

During that winter I cleaned out mom's house, attic to basement. I was there almost daily and, of course, I would put food out for Sammy even though I didn't always see him. I just assumed he was doing okay. When I did see him again that next spring, he looked terrible. He was so emaciated, and his fur was so clumped and tangled together from his front to his back paws, he could hardly walk. It looked painful for him to even move.

I felt sorry for him and I knew I had to do something about his plight, so I grabbed a stool and got to work. I used cuticle scissors and a brush and sat down next to him while he ate. I gently began cutting off the largest clumps hoping it would give him more mobility and gradually I cut the largest tangles off that day. He was feisty and swatted at me with his paw at first when I pulled too hard, but I could sense he knew I was trying to help him because he didn't leave. A few days of this grooming went by and I could finally brush him down to his skin.

By summer, I could actually call him with a "meow" that was an imitation of his own and he would come running from different directions, out of broken garage windows or basements, over fences in yards, from under wooden porches, from alleys or from other streets between the houses. He would literally "fly" to meet me, tail up like a flag, meowing all the way until he reached me. He would let me pet him and would rub against my legs. Then I would open the door and let him into mom's place and he would head for the kitchen. He was always glad to see me.

I continued to groom him, applied flea powder, and doused his food with de-worming pills. I wiped him down with damp cloths to get rid of the dust in his fur, and wiped his eyes to get rid of mucous and soot. Then I would feed him a can of soft food and filled up dishes with dry food which he gobbled up even before I left for home. Of course when I opened the door, out he went.

Sometimes he would sit down and groom himself while my husband and I would sit on the front porch drinking a couple of beers. We watched Sammy lick his paws and clean his face over and over again. He was getting better at taking care of his appearance.

Now during this time, the neighbors were curious about Sammy and how he would respond to me. The lady next door, however, was terrified of cats. But her teenage son, Charles, would come and sit on the porch with me just watching Sammy and try to pet him. I think he hoped Sammy would one day be his cat. At first, Sammy would have no part of him —he was used to me, but gradually he accepted his hand as well.

This went on all summer and by fall my husband and I thought Sammy would have to go through a long, cold winter again. We wondered what we could do about the situation. By chance, we picked up a doghouse at a yard sale, bought hay, and a heating pad. We had formulated a survival plan for Sammy in the cold.

We put padding on the insides of the house and hay in the bottom and the top to keep the heat in when the heating pad was installed and connected. A small carpet was used as a door so Sammy could climb in and out easily and still keep out the wind. The supreme test was to see if Sammy would go inside his new shelter. Excited, we placed the house on mom's covered porch, put food and water inside and waited.

Sammy knew right away this was his place. He went in, ate his food and then curled up inside and went to sleep. We were thrilled.

Everything was perfect, we thought, until one night we showed up after dark to feed Sammy. It was later than usual, and we saw Sammy was not in his house, but on the porch steps instead. When I looked inside his house, lo and behold, there was a huge opossum hissing at me. I lifted the doghouse on the far end hoping he would slide out, but he wouldn't budge! He kept hissing at me and finally I just left him there trying to figure out what to do next.

Luckily, a neighbor told us he had been trapping opossums in his garden. He set his trap for us and caught our "squatter" relocating it to another place. Finally Sammy had his "cathouse" to himself!

All the while, though, Sammy's true disposition was revealed. He was really a gentle animal, very amicable, intelligent, and lovable. And with all the patience and attention we were showering on him, he was becoming more and more domesticated.

Then one day a few weeks later, we noticed Sammy's face was swollen and his eye closed shut. We assumed he had developed an infection in his jaw which required a visit to the clinic. The vet told us it was probably a cat fight and he needed antibiotics and eye drops. At that point, while he was sedated, he also suggested we have him neutered and immunized. I gave him the go-ahead and then I decided I had to find him a permanent home.

I was thinking about the teen next door who had taken a liking to Sammy. So I asked him if he would like to adopt him. He was ecstatic and his mom dubiously agreed to let him try to have Sammy as his pet. We brought him into their home and he was shy at first trying to hide, but he calmed down enough so we felt comfortable enough to leave him with Charles.

A couple of weeks went by and we stopped by to see how everything was going. Sammy had gained some weight and looked pretty good. His fur was black and shiny from a good diet and Charles brushing him often. He went to Charles when he called him and for the most part, looked content. He was now socialized, rehabilitated and adopted. The best part was that Sammy was rescued, and we were all very happy.

Well, nine months went by since Charles had taken Sammy in. Then in mid-summer Charles sadly told me he was going away to college upon graduation, and he could no longer care for Sammy. His mom, still afraid, couldn't handle the cat either.

Again the situation had changed and I had to find Sammy another home fast. I already had six cats of my own and Sammy wouldn't be a problem except that he had the FIV virus which is not contagious to humans—only cats. How could I put him together with my healthy cats?

I could hardly sleep over this decision. This lovable, intelligent, survivor cat had to have a home—I couldn't think of putting him down! He was so special because he was lovable and smart. How could we forget what he went through and the challenges we overcame.

And so after talking to the vet and judging Sammy's gentle disposition, I decided to try and bring Sammy to my home and put him temporarily in our attached garage. I hoped with all my heart I would be able to manage him and make him comfortable during the winter months ahead. We furnished a big cage with bedding, insulation, and another heating pad. We added a space heater for zero degree weather, and all was a "go" for winter. I realized this was a repetition of what occurred only a year before!

Amazingly, we got through the winter. A few times we actually let him in the house and he was as good as gold! He meekly went and sat by a heat vent, under the kitchen table, or by the fireplace and never attempted to mingle or fight with the other cats. In my mind, I was sure he knew this was a test. He behaved flawlessly, and by spring he was becoming a member of my growing "cat colony!" He never strayed or did anything to jeopardize his place in our home.

It's been 10 years now since Sammy came to live with us. He has never bitten or clawed at us or our cats and has grown accustomed to the routine of living here. My cats have gotten used to him, too, even though they are guarded when he walks by. He is still the intimidating, big, black, "Maxi Cat" he became on the streets of Detroit. He still nonchalantly joins them in the catnip patch in the yard.

In reality, he really is a playful, gentle giant. He trusts us implicitly, loves to be petted, is very intelligent, and knows many commands as well as his name. His golden eyes always look hopefully at whoever talks to him. He *jumps and runs like a deer just like he used to hop over the fences in Detroit —he's still a beautiful cat with a great disposition.*

Sammy has been a huge success for our family. He became socialized enough to be considered an indoor cat even though he had a very rough start. I am proud and happy to have been an advocate for him, because through it all, I learned a lot about good-hearted people and pets.

And so, life is good for us and all of our geriatric cats, but most of all, for the luckiest one, Sammy. The adage, cats have nine lives is one that fits Sammy well—he has had many adventures . . . and lives!

THE END

Snow—the

Sunshine of

Winter…

Mary Minjeur

CPSIA information can be obtained
at www.ICGtesting.com
Printed in the USA
BVHW08*1307260818
525248BV00003B/14/P

9 781949 502633